Lola

THE LADYBUG

D1511709

Written by
Sarah Brinson

Illustrated by
Fredy Mendoza

Designed by
Jenna Oakley

Illustrations by Fedy Mendoza
Art Direction and Book Design by Jenna Oakley

Wholesale Inquiries: info@gbgrouppublishing.com

www.gbgrouppublishing.com

GB Press
Powered by GB Group Creative Inc.

1800, 401 West Georgia Street
Vancouver, BC V6B 5A1,
Canada

Printed in the United States of America

This book is dedicated to every young person who has felt different or alone. Your story matters; embrace it and don't be afraid to share it with the world.

Sarah Brinson

Lola and Jake were the best of friends.

The two little ladybugs did everything together: explore, dance, make music, and go to flight school!

So of course today, the second to last day of school, Lola and Jake sat on their leaf side by side.

"Congratulations, class!" exclaimed Ms. Cocni. "You've learned how to fly, how to land, and most importantly how to survive in this big bug world!"

"Tomorrow you'll become the 1,700,021st graduating class of Newberry Sky Flight School," Ms. Cocni continued. "You'll get your ladybug spots on your backs. And tomorrow night, you'll take part in the CELEBRATION OF SPOTS TALENT CONTEST!"

Welcome!

"And I have a very special announcement too," said Principal Hopper. "This year, the winner of the CELEBRATION OF SPOTS TALENT CONTEST will receive a free trip to the *City of Lights!*"

The class gasped!

For months, all the graduating bugs had been practicing for the contest.
Lola loved singing, Jake played guitar, and they had an amazing piece
planned for the CELEBRATION OF SPOTS TALENT CONTEST!

But none of the bugs could believe their little antennae when they heard
about this year's prize. They were so excited!

"Jake, it's always been my dream to go to the *City of Lights!*"
said Lola.

"I know," said Jake. "With your voice and my guitar-playing—Lola,
we can win the trip!"

"We have to practice extra tonight!" Lola suggested.

Early the next morning, Lola's little bug eyes popped open. Excited, she pulled off her cocoon covers, zipped over to the mirror...

and gasped.

"Oh, no!" she cried. "I only have one spot."

"Dingggg-dongggg!" Jake hollered, ready to get to school.
"Come on, Lola! We're going to be late."

"Jake," Lola yelled down. "I'm supposed to have seven spots this morning, but I only have one!"

"Lola, relax," said Jake. "Your spots are probably on their way right now, just making their way up to the top. They'll be here soon. Come on, let's go!"

"Maybe Jake's right," Lola thought. "I should be patient."

So on went the two little bugs, excited for the day ahead and for their big performance that night.

Jake and Lola hurried into class, removed their leaf-packs, and hung up their sweaters. But when they turned around, all their classmates were staring at Lola.

Harlie giggled.

"One spot? That's all you got?" Dora teased.

The entire class began to chant,

One spot? That's all you got?
One spot? That's all you got?
One spot? That's all you got?

Before Jake could say anything to help his friend, she had fled the classroom.
He raced out after her but she was gone.

"What can I do to help her?" he thought. "There must be something."
And then Jake got an idea.

Meanwhile Lola flew and flew and flew, going round and round and round in circles.

"Why am I the only one in our whole class who didn't grow up and get all my spots?" she wondered, sadly. "I'm just too different. I'll never fit in!"

Finally Lola saw something in the distance.
It was red, and it was waving.

"Jake? Is that you?" called Lola.

"Lola! Thank goodness I found you! I've looked everywhere!" cried Jake.
"Look, I made this for our performance tonight."

"What is it?" Lola asked.

"It's a **One Spot Sweater**! I'm going to wear this tonight so I can be just like you!"
Jake replied. "We can call ourselves *The One Spot Wonders*."

"Jake, you're the best friend in the whole bug world!" said Lola.

The two best-bug-mates hugged. Together they flew toward the school for the CELEBRATION OF SPOTS TALENT CONTEST.

"Welcome to the CELEBRATION OF SPOTS TALENT CONTEST!" said Principal Hopper. Everyone in the audience cheered and clapped with excitement.

The contest began. There were so many great performances by the graduating students!

CELEBRATION OF SPOTS
TALENT CONTEST

JOSE
THE JUGGLER

ARGO
THE MAGICIAN

LES TWINS
THE TIGHT ROPE WALKERS

"Jake, I don't know if I can do it," whispered Lola. "I only have one spot! What will people say?"

"Lola, you can! We can do this together," Jake said. "Come on. It's our turn to perform."

A tear fell from Lola's eye. She wanted to run away, but she didn't want to let Jake down. She didn't want to let herself down!

Lola took a deep breath, wiped away her tears, and took Jake's hand. The One Spot Wonders took their places on the stage.

The lights went up, Jake began to play, and Lola sang. It was magical! Lola even ended with a twirl to show off her one spot! Everyone loved their performance.